The MOON of KYIV

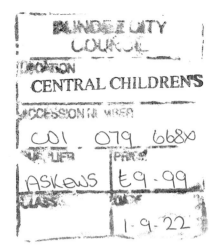
This edition first published in the UK 2022 by Walker Books Ltd
87 Vauxhall Walk, London SE11 5HJ

2 4 6 8 10 9 7 5 3 1

Original title *La luna di Kiev*
© 1980, Maria Ferretti Rodari and Paola Rodari, Italy
© 1991, Edizioni EL S.r.l., Trieste, Italy
Translation © 2022 Walker Books Ltd

The moral rights of the author and illustrator have been asserted

Printed in Malta

British Library Cataloguing in Publication Data:
a catalogue record for this book is available from the British Library

ISBN 978-1-5295-1323-3

www.walker.co.uk

Save the Children Fund is a charity registered in England and Wales (213890), Scotland (SC039570) and Isle of Man (199).

Gianni Rodari
The MOON of KYIV

illustrated by
Beatrice Alemagna

WALKER BOOKS
AND SUBSIDIARIES
LONDON · BOSTON · SYDNEY · AUCKLAND

Who knows if
the moon of Kyiv

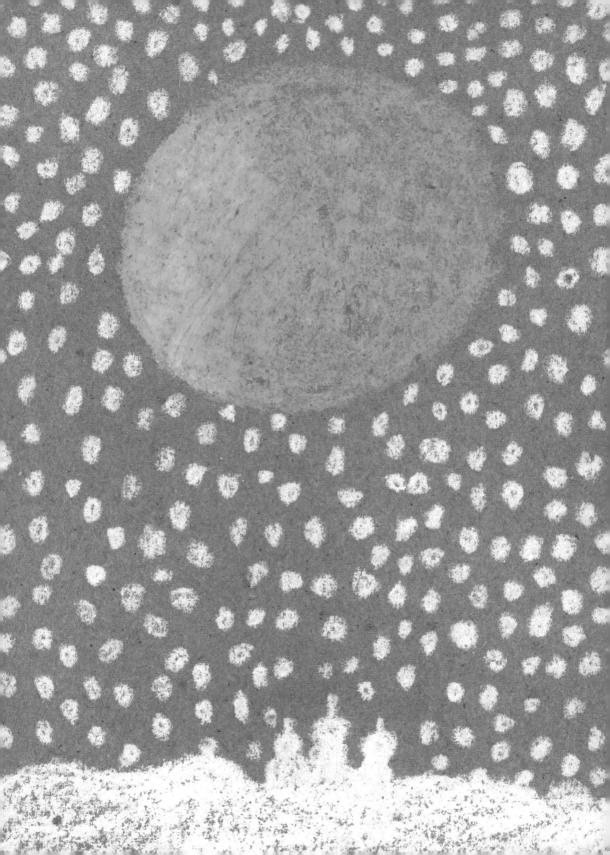

is as beautiful as
the moon of Rome,

who knows if
it's the same moon
or the sister of the
moon, perhaps...

"But I'm always the same!"
the moon calls back.
"I'm not something
you can choose
or change like a hat!

I travel each night
and give everyone my light,

from India to Peru,

from the River Tiber
to the Dead Sea,

and my moonbeams
don't need passports
to travel and live free."

The *MOON* of KYIV

Who knows if
the moon of Kyiv
is as beautiful as
the moon of Rome,
who knows if
it's the same moon
or the sister of the moon, perhaps…
"But I'm always the same!"
the moon calls back.
"I'm not something
you can choose
or change like a hat!
I travel each night
and give everyone my light,
from India to Peru,
from the River Tiber
to the Dead Sea,
and my moonbeams
don't need passports
to travel and live free."

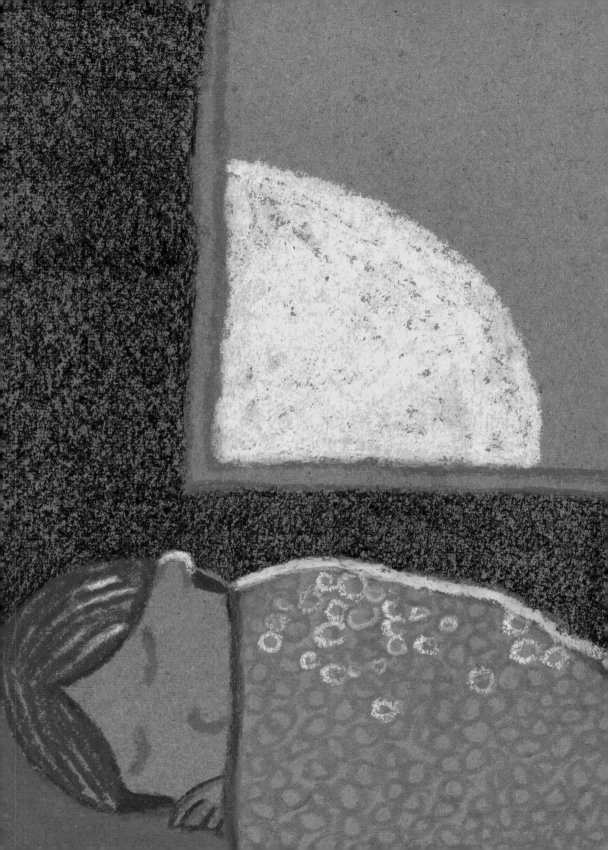

Gianni Rodari was an Italian author who worked as a teacher and journalist before writing books for children. He achieved huge success across his long career; his most significant titles include *Adventures of Cipollino*, *Gelsomino in the Land of Liars*, *Nursery Rhymes in Heaven and on Earth* and *Lamberto, Lamberto, Lamberto…* His books earned many awards and accolades, notably the prestigious Hans Christian Andersen Award in 1970. Gianni Rodari died in Rome in 1980.

Beatrice Alemagna is a best-selling author and illustrator of more than thirty books for children, including *The Wonderful Fluffy Little Squishy*, *On a Magical Do-Nothing Day* and *Harold Snipperpot's Best Disaster Ever*. She has been translated into many languages and won numerous awards, including the *New York Times* Best Illustrated Children's Book and the Hans Christian Andersen Award. Born in Bologna, Italy, she now lives in Paris, France.

Save the Children exists to make a lasting, positive difference for, and with, children, so that every child gets a fair chance of a future they deserve. Covid, the climate crisis and increasing conflict are putting children at extreme risk and we are finding new ways to support the children who need us the most.

In more than 100 countries around the world, from Afghanistan to Myanmar to the UK, we help children stay safe, healthy and learning.

We are working to find children fleeing the Ukraine crisis a safe space to live and 100% of the net profit from the sale of *The Moon of Kyiv* will be donated to Save the Children Fund for supporting children impacted by the conflict in Ukraine.

Save the Children

Save the Children Fund is a charity registered in England and Wales (213890), Scotland (SC039570) and Isle of Man (199).